Shh!
Can you
keep a secret?

You're about to meet the
Ballet Bunnies, who live hidden
at Millie's ballet school.

Are you ready?

Tiptoe this
way. . . .

Meet the Ballet Bunnies

Dolly

You'll never meet a bunny who loves to dance as much as Dolly.

Fifi

If you're in trouble, Fifi is always ready to lend a helping paw!

Pod

Pod loves to build
things out of the bits
and pieces he finds. He
also loves his tutu!

Trixie

Yawn! When she's
not dancing, Trixie
likes curling up and
having a nice snooze.

For Finn

This is a work of fiction. Names, characters, places, and incidents either are the product of the author's imagination or are used fictitiously. Any resemblance to actual persons, living or dead, events, or locales is entirely coincidental.

Text copyright © 2022 by Swapna Reddy
Cover art and interior illustrations copyright © 2022 by Binny Talib

All rights reserved. Published in the United States by Random House Children's Books, a division of Penguin Random House LLC, New York. Originally published in the United Kingdom by Oxford University Press, Oxford, in 2022.

Random House and the colophon are registered trademarks and A Stepping Stone Book and the colophon are trademarks of Penguin Random House LLC.

Visit us on the Web!
rhcbooks.com

Educators and librarians, for a variety of teaching tools, visit us at
RHTeachersLibrarians.com

Library of Congress Cataloging-in-Publication Data is available upon request.
ISBN 978-0-593-30578-2 (trade) — ISBN 978-0-593-30579-9 (lib. bdg.) —
ISBN 978-0-593-30580-5 (ebook)

MANUFACTURED IN CHINA
10 9 8 7 6 5 4 3 2 1

This book has been officially leveled by using the
F&P Text Level Gradient™ Leveling System.

Ballet  Bunnies

Trixie Is Missing

By Swapna Reddy

Illustrated by Binny Talib

A STEPPING STONE BOOK™

Random House 🏠 New York

Chapter 1

"Come on, Mom," Millie squealed with excitement.

Miss Luisa's School of Dance was having a showcase at the town hall. The dress rehearsal was that afternoon. They had to pick up Millie's costume and sequins for the show. Then Mom had promised Millie that they would go for a hot chocolate at their favorite café.

But first, Millie had to pick up four very important guests for their day out. Four very important Ballet Bunny guests.

"I'm coming." Mom laughed as she hurried down the stairs. A very excited Millie was waiting impatiently on the landing.

Mom grabbed Millie's hand and spun her around, and they danced out the doorway.

They skipped all the way up the road and straight through the doors of the dance school. Mom went to find Miss Luisa to pick up Millie's costume, and Millie took the chance to sneak into the studio. This was where Millie had first met the little Ballet Bunnies, who had since become good friends. There she found Fifi, Dolly, Pod, and a very sleepy Trixie waiting for her at the edge of the stage. All four bunnies jumped with excitement, their long, silky ears flopping around as they spotted Millie.

"Oh, bunny fluff!" Fifi exclaimed. "I love going out for the day."

"Mom promised we could get hot chocolates once we've picked up sequins for my costume," Millie said with a grin.

"It's not a day out without hot chocolate," Dolly sang as she pirouetted around Millie's bag.

Millie scooped up the bunnies into a ginormous hug, then set them back down on the stage by her bag. Dolly looped paws with Fifi and twirled her around as she sang out her hot chocolate song.

"Hot chocolate, hot chocolate,
Oh, it's not a day out without
hot chocolate!

"Hot chocolate, hot chocolate,
Oh, we all love hot chocolaaaaate!"

Millie giggled as Fifi joined in with Dolly's hot chocolate song and the two bunnies hopped into her backpack.

"All aboard!" Pod called as he climbed up Millie's arm and along her shoulder, to take a seat in the hood of her jacket.

"You're wearing your lucky hair clip," Pod said, spotting the fluffy clip the bunnies had given Millie at the start of her dance lessons.

"It's my favorite," Millie said, gently tapping the hair clip. "Whenever I wear it on stage, it feels like you are all dancing with me."

She patted Pod on his head as he nestled

into place, and then she reached down toward the smallest of the bunnies.

"And where would you like to sit today?" Millie asked Trixie, who yawned so loudly that she almost made Millie yawn too.

"I'm so tired today, Millie," Trixie said, stifling another yawn. Her eyelids drooped shut as Millie stroked her soft, gray fur. "Can I go somewhere cozy where I can take a long nap?"

"I know just the place," Millie said, and she placed Trixie in the fleece-lined pocket of her bag.

Millie held a finger up to her lips so the other bunnies knew not to wake Trixie. They all quickly ducked out of sight as the studio door swung open.

"Come on, Millie," Mom said with excitement.

"I'm coming." Millie laughed as she hurried out of the studio.

10

Chapter 2

The next stop for Mom and Millie was the costume shop. It was the best place for sequins, and it was one of their favorite stores. The shop was packed full of fabrics and hats and costumes on long racks that stretched the entire length of the store.

Mom and Millie headed straight for the huge fluffy feathers by the bead display. They threw on matching feather boas and floppy hats before striking poses in front of the store mirror.

14

"Oh, Millie," Mom said. She laughed as Millie piled on hat after hat after hat until she was mainly just a stack of hats.

As Millie put away the hats, Mom went off to find sequins for Millie's tutu. Once Millie had finished, she and the bunnies headed to the back of the store.

"Look at all these ribbons," Dolly squealed, jumping out of Millie's bag.

The back wall of the shop, draped in satin ribbons of every color, reminded Millie of a rainbow after a downpour. Dolly leapt onto the countertop by the wall and grabbed the end of a purple ribbon, wrapping it around her waist. Pod hopped to the other side of the wall and tied the end of a green ribbon to his paw. Fifi didn't want to miss out on the fun, so she jumped over too, and pulled down the end of a yellow ribbon. The three bunnies danced in and out and over and under, creating their very own maypole.

"I could spend all day here," Dolly said. She hopped over to the nearby shelf and bounced into the stacks of tutus, disappearing into the soft folds of shimmery tulle.

"But what about our hot chocolates?" Millie asked.

"Oh, bunny fluff!" Dolly cried. Nothing in the world could keep a bunny away from hot chocolate. "Let's go!" she said, pulling Pod and Fifi after her.

The bunnies hopped back into Millie's bag. Millie followed Mom out of the costume shop to the café.

◦ ✳ ◦

The café was right by the town's theater, and its walls were covered in pictures of dancers and musicians. Millie loved looking at all the drawings and paintings.

Mom went to the counter and ordered hot chocolates for both of them. Millie showed the bunnies her favorite pictures on the wall.

"It just looks like a swirl of white paint," Pod said as Millie pointed to a painting.

"It's a dancer," Millie replied. "A ballerina in the middle of a pirouette."

"You're right!" Fifi said, tilting her head. "I see her now!"

Mom was heading back to the table with the hot chocolates, so Millie quickly took a seat. When Mom went to get napkins, Millie carefully tipped out a little of her drink into her saucer for the bunnies. She placed it on the chair next to her. Then she pulled the chair in tight so Mom wouldn't spot the bunnies lapping up the hot chocolate.

"Mmmm," Dolly said, her whiskers dripping with chocolate. "Delicious!"

"What was that?" Mom asked as she sat down.

Millie froze, sure that Mom had discovered the bunnies.

But just as she opened her mouth to try to explain the talking bunnies hiding under the table, drinking hot chocolate out of a saucer, the door to the café swung open.

"Millie!" a voice called.

It was Samira, Millie's best friend from ballet class.

"We are going to the park before rehearsal," Samira said. "Do you want to come?"

Millie looked at Mom and nodded eagerly.

"Sure." Mom smiled. "Let's get these hot chocolates to go!"

Chapter 3

Millie and Samira skipped all the way from the park to the town hall. Their cheeks were red from running up and down the slide the wrong way and seeing who could swing high enough to touch the sky. They chattered excitedly about the show nonstop.

The Ballet Bunnies stayed out of sight at the park, playing nearby in the long grass. They ran up and down a tree stump and then hopped as high as they could to see who could go as high as Millie on the swings.

The bunnies even joined in from afar when Millie and Samira practiced their steps in the park before the big rehearsal. Then they followed Millie, Samira, and the moms all the way to the town hall.

At rehearsal, Millie's and Samira's moms waved goodbye to the girls and took a seat with the other parents. Millie and Samira joined the rest of their class as Miss Luisa talked to the students.

Once it was time to take the stage, Millie trailed behind her class. She wanted to be far enough away that she could talk to the Ballet Bunnies without anyone seeing.

"Good luck, Millie," Dolly whispered as Fifi and Pod gathered in close for a hug.

Millie grinned at the bunnies. She had been part of a few performances now but still felt nervous. Having the Ballet Bunnies there made the nerves a little less of a problem each time.

As the music played, Millie and her class danced the steps they had been taught. All the practicing made Millie feel very confident. She kept her chin up and didn't have to look down at her feet once.

Out of the corner of her eye, Millie could see the other dancers moving in perfect time with her, and she couldn't stop smiling.

"Lovely job, everyone," Miss Luisa

praised. "All your hard work is paying off."

The next part of the routine involved retracing their dance steps back to where they had started. Millie had always found this a bit tricky, but she took a breath, focused, and found she didn't miss a step.

"Well done, Millie," Miss Luisa said at the end of rehearsal. "That was your best performance yet."

Millie felt so proud.

Chapter 4

"Make sure you have all your stuff before you leave, children," Miss Luisa called out. "Tomorrow is the big show!"

As the children took their costumes and said goodbye to one another, Millie found herself alone at the side of the stage. She picked up her costume and jacket and packed her bag.

"My lucky hair clip!" she exclaimed, patting her hair.

"What's wrong, Millie?" Fifi asked, hopping over with Dolly and Pod.

"I can't find my hair clip," Millie said.

She emptied her backpack and carefully sifted through her things. There was her hairbrush, her hair ties, her spare tights, and her water bottle. But no hair clip.

"It must have fallen somewhere," Dolly said. "We'll help you find it."

The bunnies hopped off in different directions as Millie searched her bag and costume again.

Dolly rifled under the props on the stage. But there was no lucky hair clip there.

Pod rummaged at the side of the stage. He found an abandoned sock and three hair ties but no lucky hair clip.

Fifi looked at the front of the stage. She

searched among the lights and the rails but didn't find the lucky hair clip either.

All three bunnies rushed back to Millie's side.

"I don't know where it is," Millie said tearfully. She couldn't bear to search her

bag another time, but she didn't know where else to look.

"Don't worry, Millie," Pod reassured her. "Four sets of eyes are better than one, and five sets of eyes are even better than four."

"Oh, bunny fluff," Fifi said. "You're right, Pod! Let's wake up Trixie and get an extra set of eyes to help."

The bunnies jumped over to Millie's bag where Dolly carefully pushed open the zipper and burrowed inside.

"Trixie?" she called gently, hoping not to wake the little bunny with too much of a start.

She peered in the bag some more before whipping around to face the others.

As she looked at Millie, Fifi, and Pod, her face paled and her eyes grew wide with shock.

"Oh, bunny fluff!" Dolly gasped. "Trixie's missing too!"

Chapter 5

"Millie, what's wrong?" Mom asked as she spotted Millie frantically searching her bag again.

The bunnies hopped out of sight as quick as a flash.

"I can't find Trixie!" Millie blurted out.

"Who's Trixie?" Mom replied, confused.

41

Millie gulped. She had completely
forgotten only she knew about the Ballet
Bunnies.

"Trixie is my . . . my . . ." Millie paused.

"My lucky hair clip," she added quickly.

"Oh, Millie," Mom said, scooping her up in a big hug.

"I can't do the show without her," Millie cried. "I mean *it*. I can't do the show without it."

"Have you taken a good look around?" Mom asked.

"Yes. I've looked everywhere. It's completely lost," Millie said, tears starting to roll down her cheeks. "It's all my fault."

Mom wiped away the tears from Millie's cheeks and smoothed back her hair. "Sometimes things get misplaced, but it's okay," Mom said. "It's no one's fault."

Mom checked the stage and the props. She rummaged through the piles of costumes. She looked up and down the corridor and checked in Millie's bag too,

but she couldn't find Millie's lucky hair clip either. She put Millie's belongings back into her bag as Millie copied Mom, searching the stage, the corridor, and the costumes. "Maybe you dropped it on your way here," Mom suggested to Millie.

Millie couldn't focus on what Mom was saying. Her mind whirred. She felt frightened at the thought of Trixie being somewhere unfamiliar all alone.

Mom took Millie's hands in hers, bringing Millie's worried mind back to where they were. "When I lose something, I find retracing my steps helps," Mom said.

"Retracing your steps?" Millie repeated.

"Yes." Mom nodded. "I think about

where I have been and I follow my steps back."

"Like in the dance routine?" Millie asked, confused.

"Exactly!" Mom said. "Your hair clip is clearly not here, and you definitely had it when we left home this morning." She pulled Millie to her feet and swung Millie's bag over her shoulder. "If we follow our steps to where we were last, we might find it along the way." She hugged Millie close. "We'll retrace our steps just like in your dance routine. Don't worry, Millie."

Chapter 6

"Where do we need to go first?" Mom asked.

Millie thought hard. "We need to go to the park!" she cried. "That was the last place we were before we got to the town hall!"

"Good memory, Millie," Mom said.

Millie pushed Mom ahead of her, giving

Dolly, Pod, and Fifi a chance to climb into her bag and out of sight.

"Let's go!" the bunnies urged Millie. But she needed no encouragement at all. She had to find Trixie.

In the hallway, Millie ran fast, pulling hard on Mom's hand and dragging her out the front doors toward the park.

"Slow down, Millie," Mom said. "We might miss something."

Millie stopped and looked around her feet.

"We have to retrace our steps just like in the dance routine, remember?" Mom explained. "Let's look carefully along the route we took."

Millie glanced up and down the pavement. She thought back to her and Samira skipping along earlier that day. She didn't recognize the trash can or the blue mailbox. Of course! They hadn't gone that way at all! That's why it looked unfamiliar. They had *crossed* the street in front of the town hall.

"We need to go back across the street," she exclaimed.

"That's right, Millie," Mom said.

Millie crossed the street with Mom, keeping an eye on traffic, while Mom also looked around their feet for the lost hair clip.

Once they were safely across, Millie and Mom followed their steps back toward the park. Mom combed the pavement for the lucky hair clip, and Millie searched for little Trixie.

They followed their steps back toward where Millie and Samira had practiced their dance. They followed their steps back to the swings and then to the slide where Millie had run up and down the wrong way. They followed their steps back toward the entrance of the park by the café. But there was no sign of Trixie anywhere.

"Not here," Millie said to Mom, her voice small and quivering.

"Don't worry," Mom reassured her. "Let's just keep following our steps back."

Millie nodded, and they went to the café.

Millie remembered exactly where she and the bunnies had had their hot chocolates. She was about to rush over when

she remembered she needed to follow her steps back in the right order. So she carefully passed the paintings she had seen that morning and then checked under the tables and chairs before arriving back at the table where they had sat.

But Trixie was nowhere to be found.

Chapter 7

Millie's mind reeled with fear.
What if Trixie was lost? What if she was all
alone and frightened?

Mom asked the waitress if she had seen
a lucky hair clip, but the waitress had not.
Mom saw Millie's face fall at the news and
her eyes well with tears again.

"Don't worry, Millie," Mom said soothingly. She held up her small shopping bag full of sequins. "We still have one more place to follow our steps back to."

The costume shop!

Millie and Mom thanked the waitress and hurried out of the café, almost tripping over the steps.

They followed the route they had taken

earlier, all the way back to the costume shop. Along the way, Millie searched the pavement. She worried that Trixie had fallen from her pocket and hurt herself.

But there was still no sign of Trixie.

When Millie and Mom arrived at the costume shop, Mom talked to the owner and asked if any lost items had been handed in. Millie retraced her steps back to the ribbon wall where the bunnies had danced their maypole dance.

As Millie made her way toward the hat stand, a sound caught her ear. She stopped and listened hard.

There it was again!

It was a quiet hum, like the gentle buzz of a little snore.

Millie shut her eyes so she could concentrate on the sound.

This time she was sure of what she was hearing.

It was the sound of a sleeping Ballet Bunny.

Tucked up in the soft felt of an upturned cowboy hat was a little gray Ballet Bunny, sleeping peacefully with her paws wrapped around a very lucky hair clip.

Millie had found Trixie.

Chapter 8

Millie almost screamed with glee at the sight of Trixie balled up, fast asleep. But she knew better than to cause a commotion and have Mom running to the scene. And she definitely knew better than to startle a sleeping bunny.

Millie gently reached into the hat and gave Trixie a stroke.

"Trixie?" Millie said gently. "It's time to wake up."

Trixie yawned and stretched out her legs. "Millie!" she exclaimed. "Where are the others?"

Millie couldn't help the tears of relief that rolled down her face. It had been quite the day.

"Trixie! I've been looking for you everywhere!" she said.

Trixie could see how upset Millie was. "Oh, bunny fluff. I'm so sorry, Millie," she said quietly.

"Where have you been?" Millie asked, wiping at her tears with her sleeve.

"I've been here the whole day," Trixie explained. "When we got to the shop this morning, I heard the other bunnies dancing by the ribbons and I woke up. I got out of my cozy pocket and decided to explore the shop. But when I came back, you were all gone." The little bunny stared down at her paws. "I should've told you I was exploring. I'm very sorry, Millie." Trixie looked up at her. The tiny bunny did look awfully sorry. "I knew I should stay put in case you came back to look for me," Trixie continued. "And you did!"

Millie smiled. "That was the right thing to do, Trixie."

"Trixie!" Fifi exclaimed as she, Dolly, and Pod hopped out of Millie's bag. "We were so worried about you."

"Trixie, you shouldn't wander off like that," Dolly scolded her. Then she gave her a big hug. "I'm so glad Millie found you."

"Me too," Trixie said, smiling.

Millie and Pod told Trixie all about how they had searched the town hall after

rehearsal and how Millie and Mom had followed their steps back to the costume shop. "I was so scared when I couldn't find you. I thought you were sleeping in my bag," Millie said.

"Well, I was asleep," Trixie said. "Just not in your bag!"

Millie stroked Trixie's long silky ears and nuzzled in close. "I'm very glad you're safe."

Trixie grinned and hopped over to the hat to fetch Millie's hair clip.

"Where did you find this?" Millie exclaimed.

"It was in a stack of hats," Trixie said. "I thought it looked like yours so I held on to it for you."

"Thank you, Trixie," Millie said, fixing the clip back in her hair. She gathered up the bunnies. "I think it's time we got you back in my bag."

She tucked Trixie into the cozy pocket of her bag as Dolly, Fifi, and Pod climbed into Millie's pockets and hood. The five friends headed back to the front of the store where Mom was waiting.

"You found your hair clip, Millie!" Mom said, giving her a big hug. "It certainly is a lucky clip."

And Millie couldn't have agreed more.

Chapter 9

Millie and the bunnies couldn't wait for the show the next day. They had gone straight home to Millie's house from the costume shop. And at home, Millie, Dolly, Fifi, and Pod had been sure not to let Trixie out of their sight for one moment.

The next morning, the bunnies helped Millie practice her routine before the show. They had been a great help, and Millie couldn't wait to perform the dance onstage with her class.

Millie now knew how to get to the town hall, since she had followed her steps back so carefully the day before. So she led the way with the bunnies safely tucked in her bag and Mom close behind.

At the side of the stage, Mom kissed Millie and wished her good luck. Then she joined the other parents in the audience. As soon as she had gone, Miss Luisa called all the children to the stage.

"It's time for you to dance," Pod said to Millie.

Millie pinned her lucky hair clip onto her costume. Then she hugged each of the bunnies and waved goodbye so they could find a good spot in the audience to watch.

78

"Good luck," Trixie whispered to Millie before she headed off with the others.

It was Millie's big moment. She took a breath and stepped out onto the stage with

her class. The music started, and the lights brightened. Millie held her head high, confident and proud. She never missed a beat. She couldn't believe how far her dancing had come since her very first lesson at Miss Luisa's School of Dance. Her chest swelled with pride. Onstage, she looked and felt like a real dancer.

But she couldn't have done it by herself.

She spotted Mom whooping and cheering her on from the audience. And then Millie spotted four more familiar faces in the crowd. Four familiar bunnies.

Millie's smile stretched from ear to ear as she took a curtsy and saw the bunnies cheer for her. Then she saw the bunnies pirouette in perfect time with one another and jeté off toward the side of the stage, ready and waiting with big bunny hugs for her. Because, after all, how else would good friends end a wonderful ballet day?

Basic ballet moves

First position

Second position

Third
position

Fourth
position

Fifth position

Glossary of ballet terms

Arabesque—Standing on one leg, the
dancer extends the other leg
out behind them.

Barre—A horizontal bar at waist
level on which ballet dancers rest
a hand for support during certain
exercises.

Demi-plié—A small bend of the knees, with
heels kept on the floor.

En pointe—Dancing on the very tips of the
toes.

Grand jeté—A leap in which the dancer
throws one leg forward and the other leg
backward, so that they are in a full split
in midair.

Grand plié—A large bend of the
knees, with heels raised off the floor.

Jeté—A leap in which the dancer throws
one leg to the front, side, or back.

Pas de deux—A dance for two people.

Pirouette—A spin made on one foot,
turning all the way around.

Plié—A movement in which the dancer
bends the knees and straightens them
again while the feet are turned out and
heels are kept on the floor.

Relevé—A movement in which the dancer
rises on the tips of the toes.

Sauté—A jump off both feet, landing in the
same position.

Twirl and spin with the Ballet Bunnies in these adventures!